Magic Poems

Selected and Introduced by
Veronica Esagui

PAPYRUS PRESS, LLC

West Linn, Oregon, USA

Magic Poems

Library of Congress Control Number: 2024905733
ISBN 979-8-9906368-0-4

Book Cover Photo Credit: Mary Lowd
Graphics Book Designer: James M. McCracken
Editing: Veronica Esagui, John C. Fraraccio, and Genene Valleau

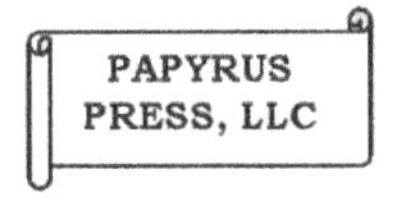

To order additional copies contact
www veronicaesagui.com

Printed in the USA

Magic Poems

Library of Congress Control Number: 2024905733
ISBN 979-8-9906368-0-4

Book Cover Photo Credit: Mary Lowd
Graphics Book Designer: James M. McCracken
Editing: Veronica Esagui, John C. Fraraccio, and Genene Valleau

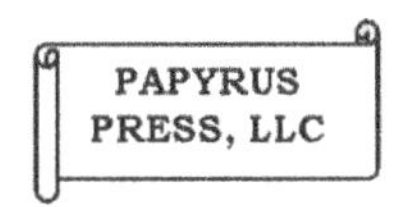

To order additional copies contact
www.veronicaesagui.com

Printed in the USA

Dedication

To Rilee, may you always find your way to the things that make you happy, and that you never lose sight of your dreams. You are a bright and beautiful soul, and I know that you are capable of achieving anything you set your mind to.

Acknowledgments

ALEXANDRA MASON is a proud daughter of Salem, OR, the Eden at the end of the Oregon Trail, who has lived a life devoted to reading, writing, teaching, and publishing. In addition to scholarly work, she has authored two experimental volumes of poetry, *Lost and Found* and *Poems Along the Way* (modern versions of ancient Chinese classics), two imaginative novels, a critical study of money and economic metaphors in the works of Shakespeare (a standard in criticism), and most recently a collection of philosophical self-help essays on the power of love in our lives, *A Handbook for Love*.

Alexandra's poems and essays have won several awards and are widely published in journals and anthologies, including *Shakespeare Quarterly, Thresholds, The Oregonian, Groundwaters, Oregon Stories, Verseweavers* and *Thresholds*. Her work is on the haiku wall in Bend, OR. She is Founder of the Northwest Poets Concord, recipient of an ACLS fellowship and an Oregon Literary Arts Award and has been named an Oregon Legacy Author. Now an emerita dean and professor at Eastern Oregon University, she is a student of bass guitar, a regular walker of the central Oregon coast, and an avid gardener who believes in magic.

alexandramasonbooks.com

Alexandra writes: *People are often at first perplexed by poetry and then say they don't much like it but it takes a certain mindset and an openness to—are you ready for this?—the art of magical transformation through language. For that is what poetry does. It moves, by virtue of its linguistic tools of simile and metaphor and all their variations to transforming something seemingly mundane into a new understanding of its significance.*

With simile, we compare things to other things: love is like a steam bath.

With metaphor, things actually BECOME other things, so that we can apprehend them more clearly: hate, a maggot gnawing at the soul. So, by definition, POETRY IS LINGUISTIC MAGIC. We unsettle the prosaic through other poetic devices like rhythm and rhyme, condensed sentence structures, and precise choice of beautiful and sometimes unusual words.

We can feel the heft of the language of poetry in our mouths, as if it is incantation, another link with the magical.

A great poem will enact a magical transformation within its lines.

AMALIE RUSH HILL is a poet, artist, and advocate for ecological, social, political, and economic justice. A prolific poet, she is working on several poetry collections. Her poetry can be found in six anthologies and in her book of poetry *The House on Prune Alley.* Amalie's critically acclaimed sci-fi series includes: *Ambolaja: Into the Light, Discontinuity, The Shoals of Time* and *Z'Torr* to be released in the summer of 2024.

She is currently writing *Time Weavers*, the fifth sci-fi novel in the Ambolaja Series.

bobhillpublishing.com

Amalie writes: *Before I learned to read I'd scribble on paper and then tell my mother the story I wrote. After I learned to read, life suddenly became larger and more interesting. I wrote my first short story in grade school when I learned about quotations marks, and also my first poem. I write every day and am now working on my fifth novel as well as poetry, short stories and essays—it's what I do!*

With metaphor, things actually BECOME other things, so that we can apprehend them more clearly: hate, a maggot gnawing at the soul. So, by definition, POETRY IS LINGUISTIC MAGIC. We unsettle the prosaic through other poetic devices like rhythm and rhyme, condensed sentence structures, and precise choice of beautiful and sometimes unusual words.

We can feel the heft of the language of poetry in our mouths, as if it is incantation, another link with the magical.

A great poem will enact a magical transformation within its lines.

AMALIE RUSH HILL is a poet, artist, and advocate for ecological, social, political, and economic justice. A prolific poet, she is working on several poetry collections. Her poetry can be found in six anthologies and in her book of poetry *The House on Prune Alley.* Amalie's critically acclaimed sci-fi series includes: *Ambolaja: Into the Light, Discontinuity, The Shoals of Time* and *Z'Torr* to be released in the summer of 2024.

She is currently writing *Time Weavers*, the fifth sci-fi novel in the Ambolaja Series.

bobhillpublishing.com

Amalie writes: *Before I learned to read I'd scribble on paper and then tell my mother the story I wrote. After I learned to read, life suddenly became larger and more interesting. I wrote my first short story in grade school when I learned about quotations marks, and also my first poem. I write every day and am now working on my fifth novel as well as poetry, short stories and essays—it's what I do!*

C. STEVEN BLUE is an award-winning poet, author, artist, musician and publisher, as well as a producer and host of literary and arts events, paying it forward by giving opportunities to other creators. Steven has eight published books, and his work is widely published nationally and abroad. Retired from a 27-year career in stage production in Hollywood, CA, Steven lives in Eugene, OR, where he continues to pursue his artistic endeavors.

wordsongs.com

C. Steven writes: *I started writing poetry as a young boy, winning my first poetry award at age 12. Poetry has just poured out of me in a natural way since then, which is why they call me a natural poet. At first, poetry was a means of pouring out my feelings, like journaling, in my dysfunctional and disintegrating family. I kept my poems in a secret journal under my mattress for most of my youth. As a result, poetry has always had a deep meaning for me. I like all forms of poetry, but am especially drawn to personal, confessional poems, because I realize what a release and comfort it is for the people who write that way.*

About my two poems in this book: "The Prescient View" is about my ability in the 1960s to recognize what new rock-n-roll songs would be huge hits before they became so, the ability to recognize new trends, ideas, and social events, much before my friends or the general public did. There were others with this ability, but the magic of foretelling new things was strong in me ... and now that magic is for the youth of this new generation.

"The Faith To Believe Magical Things Happen" is about what faith and grace really mean, no matter what your beliefs, principles, or religion are.

GENIE GABRIEL is the author of 23 published books in a number of genres that incorporate her love of animals and belief in miracles. She lives and gardens on a small farm in the Pacific Northwest with a menagerie of animals who constantly teach her some of life's most valuable lessons. For excerpts from each of her books, including paranormal adventures in *The Collie Chronicles,* please visit her website.

GenieGabriel.com

Genie writes: *The way poetry came to me is magic! Veronica asked ... and poems flowed from my heart and head ...like this:*

The way poetry came to me is magic! Veronica asked...and poems flowed from my heart and head...like this:
I didn't know I was a poet
until a friend challenged me to own it
So I wrote an ode
that reflected the love of my abode:
A farm and critters.
It seemed to flow from my heart

can't stop once I started
Now I'm hooked on rhymes
and write poems all the time.

HOPE HILL is a former foster kid who writes poetry, speculative fiction and anything else that catches her fancy. Her first poem *One Touch* was published in 2005 and since then she has authored the following books, *Dancing on the Ceiling, Secrets Under the Skin, Dancing in a Minefield* and *Into The Shadow Realms - Book 1.* You can find Hope's books on Amazon.com.

Hope writes: *When I wrote Ordinary Magic, I was inspired by the idea of magic existing in our world so I tried to think of things that feel magical and fill me with awe.*
The second poem Everyday Spells I played with the same theme but I focused on everyday rituals and labeled them spells.
I enjoyed celebrating the bits of magic in mundanity with these poems.

JEAN SHELDON has dabbled in the creative arts for much of her life. These experiments in art, poetry, mystery novels and music instilled optimism and the belief that a peaceful, united humanity is a possible and most worthy endeavor.

Jeansheldon.com

JEFFREY ROSS is a retired community college English instructor who worked for 30 years at Central AZ College. He states that his career was rewarding (and fun). Most of his teaching was comprised of "English 101-102," the composition courses nearly all college students complete. His book *Dr. Hill's Poet* is about a couple who falls in love through writing poems. In that book, he shows the connecting and sustaining power of heartfelt love poetry. Cassie and Sam's poems nurture them even though "society" is critical of their relationship (age differences and social status).

facebook.com/copperfieldpublishing

Jeffrey writes: *Poetry has always been interesting to me, probably because of the many courses I took in college involving Walt Whitman—the great compiler of images.*

I'm convinced poetry provides for a pure, distilled expression of feelings that cannot be ignored. I enjoy poetry that is short, focused, and has powerful images. I love compact, potent phrasings. I usually get my own poetic ideas from an intersection of emotions and images... if the two compliment (complement, too) each other...

POEM. And yes, most certainly, MAGIC!

I believe poetry creates a portal for transmitting feelings and ideas which would otherwise be "stifled" by text with standard grammar and syntax.

"That Memory" and "Grand Canyon Reverie" illustrate my interest in emotions and poetry.

JOHN C. FRARACCIO is a New Jerseyan who knows Oregon well thanks to friends. He retired from a career negotiating contracts. With poetry he feels he negotiates English.

John writes: *I hadn't written poetry since college. I know I'm only a guest here. But "Ronnie" asked. I'm grateful for the company.*

Kc GLOER poetic words and actions embody hope, love, intimacy and shining a light on a world that can often feel dark and overwhelming. *Nothing But Lace* is an interactive experience of passion poetry. She is presently finishing *Nothing but Love and Lace* and planning for 2024, *Nothing But the Moon, Nothing But the Sea*, *Nothing But Rainbows and Roses and Nothing But Fire and Desire*.

Lovegloriously.com

LAURENCE OVERMIRE is an American poet, author, actor, educator, genealogist, peace activist, civil rights, human rights and animal rights advocate and environmentalist. He is the author of 14 books including *The One Idea That Saves The World: A Message of Hope in a Time of Crisis.*

laurenceovermire.com

MARC JANSSEN has been writing poems since around 1980. Some people would say that was a long time but not a dinosaur. Early decrepitude has not slowed him down much; his verse can be found scattered around the world in places like *Pinyon*, *Slant*, *Cirque Journal*, *Off the Coast* and *Poetry Salzburg* also in his book *November Reconsidered*. Marc coordinates the Salem Poetry Project that includes a weekly reading, and the occasionally occurring Salem Poetry Festival. He was a nominee for Oregon Poet Laureate.

marcjanssenpoet.com

MARY E. LOWD is a prolific science-fiction and furry writer in Oregon. She has had over 200 short stories and a dozen novels published. Most of her work involves spaceships, talking animals, or both. Her work has won many awards, and she has been nominated for the Ursa Major Awards more than any other individual. You can read more of her poetry in *Some Words Burn Brightly: An Illuminated Collection of Poetry*.

marylowd.com

Mary writes: *My poetry is usually inspired by specific images I see. In the past, that has usually meant photographs I've taken of flowers or cute pictures of animals I've encountered online.*

Lately, though, it's meant pieces of AI art I've generated and then been inspired to accompany with words. The images you see with my two poems in this anthology were my inspiration for both poems.

MINNETTE MEADOR, red hair, blue eyes, six kids, and one slightly used husband. A wannabe hippy, want-their-money yuppie, pro musician, and actress for twenty years. She is a Native Oregonian, lover of music, beauty, and all things green. A willing slave to the venerable muse, Minnette lives in Lincoln City, OR with her husband and has replaced the children with two cats. Her latest book release is *The Dress* (Urban fairy tale).

minnettemeador-worldweaver.com

Minnette writes: *I didn't start out being a poet. Inspired by the incomparable Joni Mitchell, I taught myself to play the guitar and started my musical career. I had my first professional gig at the age of 14. My songs were sparked by the amazing musician poets of the 60s and 70s like Joni, Joan Biaz, Dillon, and so many others. Coping with a full-time career as a musician and actor, a student, and most importantly a teenager, my emotions were often high and needing release. My poems led to a lifetime of writing inspired by the pure soul that poetry stirs. I haven't written any music for a very long time, but I continue to use it every day in all the words I write, using language as my paints and my emotions as my canvas. Poetry inspires my writing every single day. I hope now that life has slowed down, poetry will once again lighten my soul. Thanks so much to Veronica for asking me. It's just what I needed.*

SHIRLEY MARC started writing poetry at age 15 and had poems published in various publications sporadically. In 2005, she self-published a poetry/photo book, *Life Sat Up One Night and Caught Me*. She also compiled as co-editor a book of her grandfather's poems *When the Shadows Are Long*. For the last few years, she immersed herself in writing haiku on many topics. She is a member of the Oregon Poetry Association and has served on the Executive Committee and as president. Find out more about Shirley by befriending her on Facebook.

Shirley writes: *I wrote "Prism" in 1976. I love butterflies and rainbows. On a rainy day the sun broke through, there was a rainbow, and some butterflies suddenly appeared in my garden. The poem came to me as if by magic.*

"Tonight I'll Remember..." came to me late on a cool evening at my home in San Diego in 1983 from an actual moment of my life.

Veronica Esagui's mother **SIMY EZAGUY** was a 20th–century Brazilian author, artist, music composer and concert pianist. She is featured in the *Dictionary of Famous Women*, along with Mother Teresa and Queen Elizabeth II. When women were expected to fulfill their destiny as housewives and mothers or enter a convent, Veronica Esagui's mother Simy excelled as a Portuguese author of several published books of poetry and short stories. Her oil paintings were featured in New York and London galleries. Her published music ranged from solos for piano and voice to full orchestra compositions. She was awarded in person the Silver Medal by the King of Spain for one of her original compositions. That particular music arrangement was many years later performed by the Metropolitan Youth Symphony of Portland, OR as the background music for Veronica's TV talk show, *The Authors' Forum*.

Veronica writes: *I believe that without love there is no magic, and that is what gave me the initiative to translate two of my mother's poems from Portuguese to English. I did my best to keep her voice, and I hope you enjoy them.*

VERONICA ESAGUI is the internationally acclaimed author of *The Scoliosis Self-Care & Resource Book* (English and Japanese), the historical novel *Mary Celeste—The Solved Mystery of a Ghost Ship*, and Veronica's Diaries and Adventure series, *The Age of Innocence, Braving a New World, Awakening the Woman Within, Angels Among Us* and *The Gift*. She was the theatre producer of the Simy Dinner Theatre Company in Howell, NJ, and the author of the musical plays: *Broadville I, II* and *III, The Time Machine*, and *The Black Panther Cried.* She co-wrote the comedy play *Aged to Perfection* which was sponsored by Fertile Ground and presented at the Lakewood Center for the Arts in Lake Oswego, OR. Some of her poems can be found in *Moments Before Midnight*, *Terra Incognita*, *Now We Heal—An Anthology of Hope, Love Poems* and *Magic Poems*.

veronicaesagui.com

Veronica writes: *After the successful publishing of Love Poems, it just seemed logical for the following anthology to be about Magic.*

Nearing the Winter Solstice

So dark it cannot be morning
yet grey light seeps under the shade
and cat issues an urgent call.
The tattoo of rain on skylights
does not pause—only varies—
for gloomy unending days, Nordic nights.
Sometimes gentle, or a regular cadence,
sometimes a frantic death metal beat
pounding like a giant's hammer,
Let me in, I'm coming in.
And it gets into your brain, this rain
and its rhythm. *Ba da bop bop bop,*
dip dip dip dippety dip.
Its great-uncle, the sea, riffs on the tune
in a curtain of sound unceasing,
before we know it
imperceptibly echoing
the flow of our blood
in our ears, the whoosh of our breath
and the l*ubba dubba squish* of our hearts.
Just when we become winter, reports say
it might end, after another warm front

with wave after wave, the high sea pounding
our soggy shore, the water puddling in any cranny,
dripping in rivulets from gutters.
And then the magic of miracle,
our sign a white garage door and a constellation of
200 minute tree frogs clinging,
so neon green they can be nothing
less than a harbinger of that first brave
leaf of spring.

Go Where I am Going

For Jean Cocteau

If you want to be truly free
you must rise each day
to a googol of choices:
whether to budge at all,
how to save yourself,
how to save the world.
Loonies endure an undetermined life—
yes to breakfast and coffee
and then and then and then?
Sages recommend a strict routine:
ablutions and meditative thoughts,
spare furnishings and order,
serenity in detachment.
Some days I want to explode
in the excesses of life:
drink Bellinis ‘til the bottle rolls on,
climb to the crown of the agéd pine,
then swim in the frigid sea.
On that beach I’ll meet a man
with laughing and sorrowful eyes,

no tattoos but scars
raised like welts or bursting seams
in hidden folds.
We know no destination
and tell our time from the sun.
As if by magic comes a pale horse.
We clamber on and jointly say these words—
Horse of freedom, horse of fate,
Go where we are going!
Wordless we three try to skirt the surf,
hooves catching in the breakers,
before us just the headland
and now what lies beyond.

They Read Fairy Tales to Us is about how we stifle and devalue the light within everyday objects, to teach children how to be adults instead of instilling them with curiosity, wonder and imagination. I'm not anti-science; in fact, I've discovered that quantum physics is as magical as anything we've ever conjured up. It's all in how you look at it. And because we'll never be able to answer every question, magic will live on in mystery, it's in all life if we take the time to see it.

Amalie

The Read Fairy Tales to Us

They read fairy tales to us
and then talked us out of them…

We had to grow up, be practical and serious, work diligently, become CPAs and attorneys, builders, toolmakers and workmen

They offered us a gift, then ripped it out of our arms because we'd aged out of childhood; we had to be sensible now, had to conform to the everyday, to a dull and plodding life based on a schedule; had to learn to be utilitarian, expected to work at useful things

And then we passed on that regimen to our own children…We banished our own yearnings, abandoned the children we had been, renounced the magic of beginnings, of possibilities and potential, of what could be instead of what could not, what would never happen

We were given magic and then burned it on the altar of adulthood, to be patience and self-restrained, an inevitability of a grim life

We must remember, it was bright magic that inspired us to become artists and poets, even astronauts; people who believed in the wonders of the world, in adventure, not humdrum; people who wanted to see beyond the mundane into marvels and spectacles, to see and feel miracles, to be awed and surprised by life, not destined to repeat everything just because it has always been that way

We've always wanted more, expected more than daily routines, life numbing normality and tedious work… If we were to become mathematicians or astronomers, we'd want to explore the beauty of numbers and equations, the mysteries of the unknown, of the cosmos, the quantum level; the places we knew we couldn't go, yet craved to be among the stars and the muons and electrons…

If we're to become writers, well, that's easy, we can take ourselves anywhere we want to go, far or near, large or small, and artists are our companions, fellow travelers, illustrating our imaginations so others might also enjoy our stories, and maybe even rediscover the child within still hoping to be released, to grasp the beauty and allure of a life lived out of bounds and then to ponder recalling that in the beginning everything was magic …

In Every Sunbeam

I've always felt a fascination with beginnings. Our ancient ancestors had ideas about why and how things were. Their vivid imaginations saw not only magic but other things that might answer questions about life.

So this kind of poem is part of me, the child I was and will always be.

Amalie

In Every Sunbeam

Yes, magic exists, surely you can see and feel it
because we all know about magic
It was real back then, at the beginning when
superstition kept it in place, corralled by sorcerers
who made it their private domain, mysterious,
sometimes dark because to live is an antonym of
evil, and an anagram of veil — spelling makes it so,
but that's not magic, it's wordplay, incantations to
make us look at the wrong hand, not the one
holding the bean or card

Wizards wanted it to be property, tamed but people
forgot to be amazed and forgot what it was at first
that it came out of the beginning

Magic lives inside every sunbeam,
it rides on the wind, sleeps in granite,
locked inside every geode and agate
Trees understand magic,
exhaling it into the atmosphere to be inhaled
by every aerobic Earthling

Magic travels on neutrinos, passing through solids and liquids —it's in us, in our atoms and cells, circulating energy and life

We don't believe in magic because we can't see it, can't see it because we stopped believing in it, but children see magic in the world before they're taught not to, when they stop asking the most important questions

You can tell magic is seeping out of the world because we no longer believe in it, or in life and wonder

When we demanded an answer to every mystery we lost the capacity to see it, to feel the magic within ourselves
It's in you and me and every molecule of life — close your eyes and there it is if you can summon enough awe; it's in every law of nature, it's what makes the world spin and the stars shine; it's in the air and soil and water — We have the power to bring it back; we need it to resuscitate the earth with one innocent act of gratitude, of empathy and love

— It's why we love fantasies — it's the magic calling out to us

Listen!

The Prescient View

I wish I could strike a flame
from those ingenious days
with a fire so high
that screams so loud
if only you'd hear what I say

Take me back to the wonder and glory
of the intuitive nature I had
sensing new things
in the rock and roll world
before their time was at hand

The magical meaning
of feeling it come
—so prescient—so furtive—so grand
with such inspiration it drove what I did
I felt that my time was at a hand

But as you grow older that magic does fade
you no longer have the clear view
into things that may come
that's reserved for the young
that magic's no longer for you

The Faith To Believe Magical Things Happen

Do you feel, sometimes,
magical, mystical moments in your life,
where it seems like something happens
that is more than coincidence?
Or you narrowly escape some catastrophe?

At those times
there is almost a spiritual presence
in your mind,
in your feelings.

This is one of the things
that draws people to religion:
seeking help in understanding,
or seeking more of that magical, mystical presence.

Grace, Guardian Angel, Fate, Destiny
—whatever you want to call it,
this is what faith is about;
those things that happen in your life
to make you feel like either
someone is watching over you,

or something is magical,
mystical, coincidental—and so on.

Whatever your faith may be,
it is about believing in something intangible,
something you cannot see or touch,
but something that touches you inside,
nevertheless.

So it is about something you believe in,
or desire to believe in,
based on those moments in your life
that happen,
that you can't explain,
that make you believe
a power greater than yourself
is at work in your life,
and maybe in everyone's life,
to make magical things happen.

I Want To Be Magic

I want to be Magic
To heal with a wave of my hand
No more wars
No anger
No hatred

No forgiveness
there is no need
for all move through this world
with peace and compassion
and greatest integrity.

I want to be Magic
filled with positive energy
Powerful and sure that all I do
will bring about the
highest good.

No homeless pets
No destruction
No abuse or hurtful words or deeds
We move among our animal friends

and plants and birds and trees
and let them live their lives
untouched by human foibles and fear and grief

We care for our Earth
our home
each other
and truly live in paradise.

Can you imagine?
Can you join with me and say,
I want to be Magic

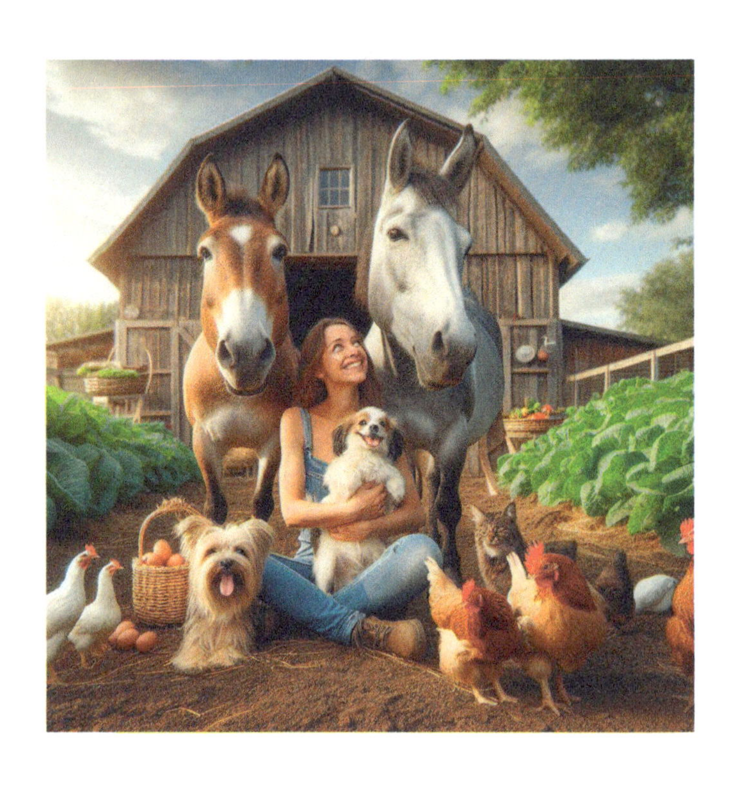

Magic on the Farm

Where is the magic?
I wanted to see
if magic was anywhere close to me.
So I went looking
and here's what I found
in everyday places here on the farm.

When my dog, Dasha, got up off the ground
And stood on four legs and walked all around.
She had not stood for many months,
yet you see
Now that she can,
That is magic to me.

The horse is fearful, they said
Doesn't like human touch
Yet his eyes drift closed
at the caress of the brush
That trust shows the magic that love can bring
A magic I cherish more than anything.

I didn't know I needed a donkey
But the angels sent to me
A handsome guy with soft gray fur
With soulful eyes and heart so pure
Magic to ease my guilt and heal my grief
and live the rest of life with me.

When dusk settles in, so do my chickens
But the ducks keep watch
and quack like the dickens
She's here! She's here!
is the message they speak
As they waddle inside
for their veggies and leaves.

My chickie girls have fluffed up their feathers
and tucked their heads and snuggled together.
In the morning they will leave me eggs
then go outside to scratch for bugs and play.
Day after day it all seems the same
But is it really?

How do they know when it's time to come in?
How do they know when the sun shines again?

For the days aren't the same
Some are short; some are long
Some are rainy and stormy
when the sun doesn't show up at all

And sometimes the moon up above shines so bright
Why don't they want back out on those nights?
Do the sounds of predators warn them to stay
Inside where it's safe and not go astray?
Yes, they are more than simple creatures,
I believe,
They are feathered magic to me.

When the moon hangs low in the midnight sky
Surrounded by stars and planets that shine
as they move in a dance of precision well timed
How do they do that? How can that be?
It surely must be magic
At least that's how it seems to me.

When the winds become warm with spring's tender promise
The rains soften and nourish the world all around us.

Seeds sprout, flowers bloom, then bear veggies to eat.
How do they do that? How do they know what to be?
Green beans or lettuce or carrots or peas
That part will always be magic to me.

Oh, there's magic around us
if only we see
with eyes full of wonder
At all that can be.

What You Have to Give

You watch as squirrels give chase,
romp and frolic in the grass
then dash away.
Now you have a smile to give.

You listen as the soft harmony
of a brook, water and stone,
recall melodies shared long ago.
Now you have a song to give.

You relax as the hushed forest
caresses you in its safe
and soothing calm.
Now you have peace to give.

Life does not ask for
more than we can give,
only that we accept
the gift of each moment,
a gift
to keep
to share

Breathless

Each day humanity
passes before me
Surprising me
Incensing me
Making me laugh
Making me cry
Each day humanity
passes before me
Leaving me breathless
in the wake
of its beauty.

Ordinary Magic

It's the first green you see
After a disaster
Wipes out everything
The moment when you know
It's all going to work out
How rainbows follow storms
And the way artists create
Something from nothing
How soup tastes better when you're sick
But best when it's homemade
It's why laughter is contagious
And kindness can save lives
That second chances exist
It's the way we band together
When the chips are down
It's the awe you feel
When you witness something
You know you couldn't do
It's the way art makes us feel things
It's the way that all things grow
And all the little things
That remind us

Life is full of ordinary magic
We just have to be willing
To look for it

Everyday Spells

Wishes on dandelions
And tuck-ins at night
New Year's resolutions
And birthday pinches
Tossing salt over your shoulder
And blowing out candles
Hanging horseshoes right side up
And picking up pennies
Wishing on shooting stars
And vision boards
Speaking things into existence
And kissing under mistletoe
Pinkie swears
And cross my hearts
Wishing at 11:11
And words of affirmation

Grand Canyon Reverie

She sat, feet dangling, on a safe ledge, lost in
dreams, at the Canyon's South Rim.
Some miles across, as a crow might fly, a man
leaned on a North Rim pine tree,
Thinking of her, of course.
She was from the Midwest.
He was from... well, it doesn't matter.
Such an epic romantic chasm between them.
Yes, the world paused and sensed their loving.
The world wanted them together.
The sky brilliant, the Canyon deep, the shadows and
hopes mysterious... well, they watched and waited,
watched and waited.
For happiness complete.

That Memory

The two of us chatting
Strolling from the restaurant
Just two of us in grand--
but weary--
cosmic focus
That memory oh...
Yes, we were
Destiny bound and seemingly
Unstoppable
Silhouetted in a desert sunset
Aloof and unapologetic
while those curious eyes watched
as we ambled eastward...
Well, the lovely memory is fading now,
No fault of ours
Just a victim of time and space and age...
Like failing eyesight
A sad erosion of what was good and loving
And we won't be going back.

The Stage Magician's Daydream

Any card, any number
I've rehearsed this for weeks
To an audience of none and a standing ovation
        each and every time
Sleight of hand, slight of mind?
That's not the way I see it
In fact I'd better not see it
I don't need any more distraction
        than I provide myself
The ensuing gasp and sound of applause
Even a loud chuckle for a suspect reason
Are enough for me

Any thought, any word
Each is as much a creative act
Neither ever comes out of nowhere
Inspiration is no disinterested party
We learned to speak before we could walk
We learned to walk before we could put
        two and two together
Someone had to help with that last part
I don't recall arguing over that

Or even wanting to know how and why
That was enough for me

Any hope, any dream
Can come out of nowhere
At least I feel better when I feel it does
It means I'm not alone and never have been
What I thought or thought I knew
What I learned and suspect I forgot
Who I met
Who I loved
It all adds up to more than the sum of the parts
That will be enough for me

Unicorns Run Free

Take me away to a wondrous land
Where fairytales live
Where we play in the sand
Take me away where unicorns run free
Where happiness breathes
Where beauty is all we see

Take me away to a place to believe
Where all is peaceful and good
Where we don't ever have to leave
Take me away to this magical place
Where bananas, lemons and pineapples flourish
Where everywhere you turn,
there is so much to taste

Take me away to a sky full of rainbows
Where they double and triple
Where they shine and glow
Take me away to beyond the horizon
Where peace and love is all we know
Where friends help friends and you're never alone
Take me away

A Fall Before Evening

Can I pull a poem out of the air
Like a magician
Catching coins
Or must I labor like Hercules
To topple the temples of the Gods
Into golden dust

I don't have a feeling for these slaughtered words
My mind half sleeping
Becomes its own allusion
A sacrifice too great for holy assurance

Break with me the rhyme of
Yesteryear
Find in the silent space between
Light and shadow
The pregnant thought that gives birth

To a language all its own.

THE MAGIC OF BELIEVING

Boy Inside

There was a boy inside me
Full of life
Full of fun
I used to see him in the mirror
Grinning impishly at me
He'd tell me secrets
Of the wildwood
And the elderberry trees
And speak of magic in the heart
Of every living thing.

'Cross the babbling brooks of time
We would skip among the shadows
Chasing unicorns and dragonflies
Through the caverns of the mind
And then we'd stop and listen
To the silence in a stone
And touch the color of the rainbow
That only blind men know.

Yes
I miss the boy inside me
I miss that foolish grin
He left without my knowing
And I'm not sure why or how

But when I look into the mirror
I only see the frown

Poem of the Ponzo Illusion

Train tracks are ladders to other places

I am now the same
Equal dimensions trapped
On a flat flat plane

Ties are less formal than rungs

Immediacy
Of distance and perspective
When I hold your hand

Both are where space and time are the same

Poem of the Moon Illusion

Horizon looms large
Shrinks as it rises, really
Though, it's the same size.

Is it our brains that trick us
with perceptions of closeness?
Is it the mystery of holding hands of looking,
finally, into each other's eyes?

Big or small it's just
Purely intellectual
The size is the same

And now my brain says you are near,
a mystery at the end of my hand.
And now you are far away while sitting,
our hips pressed accidently together.

Size consistency,
Refraction and distance, none
Come close to the truth.

Freedom is a Cat

A pair of goldfish mages
Cast their spells
And compelled
The water to form around them

A form so divine—
A most terrifying feline!
—now theirs to control
As through the neighborhood
They roam, free and
Unhindered

No longer confined
To a babbling fountain

The Robot Unicorn Solution

If magic doesn't exist
I'll make it

If the universe missed its chance
To add a dash of mystery & romance
Filling the woods with unicorns
I'll draw up plans
For artificial, mythological
Technological solutions
To fill in the gap

Perhaps robots dancing
On hooves
Is what we've always lacked

Midge, my sister-in-law, cursed with Cerebral Palsy, was a very talented savant with numbers, dates, and times. She passed away a few years ago. We loved her very much. This poem is dedicated to her amazing abilities, the innocence of her soul, and her ability to rise up against the odds with literally half a brain. I believe wholeheartedly that Midge and those like her are very special angels that inspire all they touch.

Minnette

Savant Voice

Juxtaposition'd on a burning heart,
Her innocence fell, a falling star,
Memories gone, but instincts smart,
She stumbled blind to her voice's art.

From her eyes, the fever quaked,
A wetted tear, a silver streak,
And yet inside, the bubble ached.
The magic rose however meek.

They awed at her, a golden maid,
A savant amongst the chosen few,
Her voice like golden honey laid
Across the countless, screaming crew.

And thus the great and huddled mass
Jumped to their feet and thundered hands
Against her sorrow, a sad trespass,
Voice rose like magic atop the stands.

As night came nigh, in narrowed sleep,
She whisked the dreams away,

Her magic gone, her memories seep,
She finally lost the day.

The Writer's Plight

My fingers fly like humming bees,
Ghostly gray, and sunset pink,
Across the squares to catch the tale,
Dizzy with remembrance, sad when lost.

The words like magic music flow to my brain
Telling me to seek the truth.
But truth is fickle,
Like changing tides and daily news.
Would I recognize it in the end?
Perhaps.

I sit astonished as beings jump onto the page
Like butterflies.
But who's writing who?
Is their version better than mine?
Do they comfort or control me?
It is the plight I signed up for when the muse
Dug her heels into my fate.

They change my life
Like a hard rain drowns the beetle.
They are inconsistent,
Bold liars,
Sneaky tricksters,
That battle with me whenever

I caress the keys.
I know I could kill them with two words,
but they just don't listen.

Oh great and valiant sigh,
I give way to the muse's torture
And sort them out;
Hero, heroine,
Antagonist,
Comic relief,
As I sort out life;
Mentor,
Family,
Friend,
Fiend
Comedienne.
Write it down, I cry,
The story grave, or funny,
Or poignant, yet important.

I give myself to art,
Though it kills me a little every day.
Or is it life that sucks away existence
In its vicious slothfulness?
In return, the joy of rightness
Overshadows the misery.
After all, what else would I be doing?

Tonight I'll Remember…

A pen flowing ink across a page,
a violet candle beckoning me,
marigolds in a jar–
Bright suns brought to earth.

A rumpled, striped afghan
tempting drooping eyes
with faded threads made
Of warmth and love and laughter.

Incense burning lazily
in an archaic brass burner
wafting memories of ancient temples
And insightful sages praying daily.

And your breathing, from the corner chair,
slumbering over a thought
that caught your imagination
And flew away into the night.

Prism

A glowing haze of azure wings
winking at the wind,
whirring in my ears,
makes rainbows in the rain.

Soft blues and yellows
pattern shades of green
that drip scarlet
in the night.

The butterflies
shatter their cocoons;
destroy the crystal worm
that dies for life.

Like fine Rhine wines
they pour liquid violet
into the sun.

The Seamstress

by Simy Ezaguy
Translated from Portuguese
by Veronica Esagui

Every day she looked forward
To tearing a page off the calendar
She extracted pleasure
welcoming
the new days ahead

At her old sewing machine
she greeted with a smile
the magic spark
of her dancing feet
as she peddled
along with her heartbeat
the incoming promise
that would linger
as long as she kept the sewing needle
fed with a thin thread of blue

She knew
when the hemming was finished

the material would be devoured
like Cinderella's dress
by the midnight hour

But
until then
time stood still
as her nimble fingers
imparted the magic realm
of a living memory
that could never be extinct

Same time tomorrow
they would dance again.

I feel life

by Simy Ezaguy
Translated from Portuguese
by Veronica Esagui

Remembering my first steps
running over the green meadow
kissing the wild flowers

I feel life
when I see
birds of a thousand colors
a fairytale of wings and
heartfelt emotions
much like children's laughter

I feel life
when I see the sky
in the serene light of the fields
pine trees embrace each other
in subtle breathing vibrations
naked, free, reaching up
to the heavens.

I feel life

God, light, love
when I hear the sound of a flute
announcing the magic of a new day.

An Introduction to Magic

Why do you think they named
the six-mile-long peninsula
strand of sand along
the New Jersey coast,
Sandy Hook?

No, its name is not a coincidence
it's a message from those who know exactly
where the most exquisite treasures
are cleverly hidden from the naked eye
since the beginning of time

Come
let's unfold together
the magic of the ages
buried deep by pirates
that once lived only in story books

Imagine
a single seashell laying there,
in the vastness of sand
for over a hundred years

waiting just for you
Makes you think, doesn't it?

How about that one of a kind
tiny yellow and purple pebble
stolen from a faraway kingdom
where only magicians
know where to find them

Another coincidence, you think?

Go ahead, pick it up
hold it to your heart
take the salted air in your lungs
taste the salted tears of the ocean
spraying a kiss on your face while
shamelessly embracing your feet
uncovering just for you
your most magic moment.

Abracadabra

Some say
there is no magic
without a magician
Is it because we need the illusion
to defend its reality?

Are magic moments
simply our interpretation
of what we cannot explain?

If it's only magic
how difficult can it be?
How long can it take
to learn the tricks of the shrewdest magician
to grasp what's real inside the little black box
the quick shuffling of cards
and pull out a white dove
from a bottomless empty hat?

I am ready!
Let the show begin!

No,
please
don’t tell me

Let me
read your mind!

Abracadabra!

Did you just wish
for a better world?
Sorry…
I don’t do miracles
I am only a magician.

Not By Henrik Ibsen

There was a famed author from Portugal
Who offered her novel most nautugal
        She opened a booth
        And hollered "Forsooth!"
So patrons could read what they oughtugal

Made in the USA
Monee, IL
02 May 2024

57818698R00075